Carols and Consent

A Stepbrother Reverse
Harem Romance

Carols and Consent

A Stepbrother Reverse Harem Romance

Part of the
Christmas Cherry Auction series

Sylvie Haas

Copyright

Contents

Blurb

My rockstar stepbrothers are every girl's fantasy. And if I were to reveal my naughty secret, I'd admit they're my fantasy too. But years of being used by people who simply want access to my brothers have caused me to distance myself.

Am I foolish to think the Christmas Cherry Auction will give me a moment to step free from their celebrity shadow?

Apparently, I am, because when they're supposed to be putting on a concert, they swagger into the auction. They drive the bids sky high. And they win.

Four hours of my time!

Will one night with these four heartthrobs get them out of my system, or tangle our lives forever?

If you love dirty-talking men who know how to teach their untouched stepsister a very important holiday lesson, don't miss this year's Christmas Cherry Auction!

Sensitive readers: Please be advised that this story includes a scene of consensual non-consent, also abbreviated as CNC. To be clear, the characters agree ahead of time that they want to do this and have a safety option if anyone changes their mind in the midst of the scene.

One

Big D

Smack. My phone goes tumbling to the floor as I stumble backward. It takes me a second to register that I missed the doorway into the backstage meeting room.

"I think you were aiming for that big opening, not the door jamb, slick," Jack says, as all three of my brothers laugh.

They wouldn't be laughing if they saw what I *think* I just saw. I grab my phone from the floor. Damnit. My phone turned off when it hit the ground.

"If you break your fingers walking into a door jamb, it's on *you* to tell the audience the show is canceled because our keyboard player is a dumbass."

I don't bother looking up to acknowledge Calvin, who's the oldest, and a little cocky about being lead vocals and guitar.

"Go to hell." I tap my thumb against the side of my phone. Why the fuck does it take this thing so long to power on?

Joining my brothers, I sit on a stool for our pre-concert check-in. If there are any last-minute changes, I'm fucked. The image that seared itself into my brain seconds before I ran into the door and dropped my phone is occupying all of my brain space.

"What the hell has you so flustered?" Jack asks. He's the bad boy of the band, but it's a façade.

"Hang on." I want to be sure before I say anything.

"Do we need to make a 'no phones' policy for when we're on stage?" Calvin mocks me.

The screen powers back on, saving me from arguing with him. I tap into the social media app and try to remember the name of the gossip group from the hole-in-the-wall town less than an hour away. One of our fans just invited me to it. *Smut* something.

I type *S-M*— There it is. *SmorgasSmut*.

And there she is, Aurora, our stepsister.

Not the little kid we always gave over-the-top support to. Not the gangly teen with a passion for theater. Not the bubbly, innocent sister—my brain short circuits.

Fuck-Me red lipstick, way too much for her light complexion. Long, blond wavy hair styled to perfection. And that smokey eye-makeup. Shit.

My cock forgets that she's been our sister since she was three. That we share a last name since our dad adopted her. My cock shouldn't be getting hard.

She shouldn't be wearing that sexy red and white strapless number. I shouldn't be wanting to lick up her red and white striped thigh-high stockings to find her sweet spot.

Our band's success has required us to be on the road a lot the past few years. It had helped me try to ignore how little Rory had grown into such a gorgeous woman. But damn. We're back home and she's...off limits. I know that.

The tension in my jaw is enough to trigger a headache. I shift my lower jaw from side to side, then rub a hand inconspicuously over the strain in front of my pants.

The stage manager enters and starts talking. *Yada, yada.*

I have to figure out why Rory's dressed like that, and why she's being gossiped about. I scroll to read the comments. "She's in a fucking auction?"

I almost drop my phone again.

"*She* and *auction* in the same sentence. Sounds like something I'd like." Jack steps beside me. I scroll back to the picture.

"Oh damn," he says. "That's Rory."

"Tell me something I don't know."

"She's in an auction?" Jack's as dumbfounded as I am.

Her body glitter sparkles almost as much as her light blue eyes. Will I go to hell for wanting to roll around with her and get that sparkle in inappropriate places?

Brian, the stage manager, tries to cut in. "The opening act's about to go on. Time to focus."

"Aurora's in an auction?" Calvin says coming over, ignoring Brian.

"It's some small-town thing." I'm trying to sort the details through the comments people have posted. I'm not the only one who's ready to bid on my sister.

"Shit! The auction is at a sex club." My chest tightens. No way in hell my little sister should be in a sex club. I do some mental math and confirm that she's eighteen. Not that I need to. I know the exact day she turned eighteen.

"What's the name of the sex club?" Calvin asks, his fingers poised on his phone.

"The Aubergine Affair. The winner gets four hours of help with holiday prep but apparently last year, the winners got—"

"Stop," Calvin says.

"Just telling you the facts."

"Save it for in the car. The Aubergine Affair is thirty minutes away."

"You can't leave." Brian blocks the doorway.

"Tell the opening act they're getting extra time." Calvin's never looked more serious.

"That's not how this works."

"It does tonight."

Calving reaches into the cabinet and grabs his keys. "Let's go."

We've blown past Brian and are halfway down the hall. He's pissed. "You can't just leave."

If my brothers are having the same thoughts as me, I pity anyone who tries to stop us.

Travis keeps his voice low. "What are we planning to do with her when we win her?"

"I'm sure as hell not asking her to wrap presents." Jack matches my sentiment.

Two

Aurora

"I need to help Wendy." I grab Bianca's shoulders to get her to focus. "You're raising money for the women's shelter."

I slap her butt and nudge her onto the stage.

In seconds, Wendy emerges from behind the privacy screen, holding up the front of her dress. She spins around. "Zip please."

"I've got body glitter too."

She glances over her shoulder as I zip her up. "I noticed."

"Want some?"

"Is there any left?" She laughs.

"It's possible I overdid it, but I plan to sparkle." My smile hides the frustration of never really being seen once someone hears my last name. My stepdad officially adopted me, since my dad walked out of my life when I was little, and I've lived in the shadow of my stepbrothers ever since.

Jefferson, the auction emcee, has been given strict orders not to utter Bengtsson; I'm simply Aurora tonight.

"Do you hear how much the bid's going up? This is crazy." Cindy makes sure we're listening. "Twenty-five thousand and climbing. Bianca raised the full twenty thousand."

"Is it her stepbrothers?" I dust Wendy with body glitter while she puts the cute red gloves on.

We stand side by side and check ourselves in the mirror. It was hard for me to decide which dress to wear, but the tutu style skirt won out. It's fun and helps me channel my love of theater.

I'm packing as much into tonight as possible, complete with a little song and dance number to Marilyn Monroe's *Diamonds Are a Girl's Best Friend*.

We join Cindy at the edge of the curtain. The poor girl's shaking.

I wrap an arm around her. "You're going to be fine. Those bidder paddles are hot, just like your bottom's going to be before the evening's over."

She pulls back and puts her hands over her face. "I don't know if I can go through with this."

Turning toward Cindy, I tease. "We convinced Bianca. We'll convince—"

Jefferson's voice elevates. "Going, going, gone. Bianca is sold to bidder number three."

A ruckus at the back of the room draws my attention. Leather, flannel, ripped jeans, swagger—Big D, Jack, Travis, and Calvin. I can barely breathe. "My stepbrothers..."

"What?" Cindy says. "I thought her brothers were winning?"

"No. My stepbrothers. They're here. No, no, no." The velvet curtain slips from my fingers.

Cindy says, "They have a concert tonight. They can't be here."

Wendy checks. "It's definitely them."

As she holds the curtain open, Mark growls orders at Bianca and is carrying her off the stage.

Cindy thinks fast. "Somebody grab Bianca's bag. I think they're leaving."

"All right, everybody." It's Big D's voice followed by a loud hand clap. "We've got to get back to our concert, so what's the 'buy now' price for Aurora?"

This can't be happening. Flashbacks of the high school talent show pin themselves in my brain. My helpful big brothers catcalled and cheered *before* my performance. It drew the audience's attention to them. I had to wait for their fans to calm down before performing Annie's *Tomorrow*.

It was one of the moments that led me to distancing myself from them. Along with so many times my peers pretended to be my friends in hopes of getting to meet my brothers.

Tonight was supposed to be safe. I don't want to wait until tomorrow for the sun to come out. I want to be seen for me. I grab Bianca's bag. "I'll take it to her."

I step out from behind the curtain, startled by how quickly Calvin made his way to the front. He's the oldest and always in charge. Probably barged through everyone with his lean build and broad shoulders. And if they met his gaze, yeah, he has a super power with those intense eyes.

"Sorry bro, I'm not up for bid yet. Besides, I've got to run this out to Bianca."

Calvin hops on the stage and takes the bag before I can resist. "Who can take this to Bianca? Our stage manager's already blowing up our phones. No time to waste."

"You can't just come in and change the order of the auction. Cindy is next." Annoying little sister isn't a good look or sound for me, but I'll own it.

Jefferson speaks into the microphone. "Anyone object to a 'buy now' price of five hundred thousand?"

The crowd goes wild. My head jerks toward Jefferson. He's serious.

I'm numb. My brothers can easily pay that. How can I deny the women's shelter getting such a huge donation?

Jack, the youngest, and the bad boy persona in the band, hops on stage and holds his hands to the side. "Anyone object?"

I object to him having his shirt unbuttoned. Those ripped abs and his sly smile make him irresistible.

I blink hard as he turns, extending an offer for a handshake toward Jefferson. Not again. Why won't they just let me do my thing? Channeling Marilyn, I try to own my fifteen seconds of the spotlight and I slap his hand away.

"I do! I object!"

If only the brief contact hadn't sent sparks of excitement racing through me.

"Why?" Jack's brow furrows as he rubs his other hand over the skin I touched.

"I'm supposed to have my time on stage. I'm supposed to get bid on." Pesky little sister is shining her brightest, but I applaud her for finally standing up to them.

"You want to get bid on?" An air of disbelief taints his words.

"Yes, but..." Why can't I force the rest of the thought from my mouth—*but not by them.* Now is a terrible time for my secret crushes to surface. Where are you now, pesky, defiant little sister?

Jefferson pivots. "Cindy, would you mind if Aurora goes next? And could you run this out to Bianca?"

He's keeping the show rolling, which is his job. Poor Cindy. She takes the items from Calvin and rushes outside. I hope she doesn't use this chance to back out. When the door opens, there's a deep rumble growing louder by the split second. Motorcycles. A lot of them.

Under Calvin's guidance, Travis hands a bidder paddle up to him.

Jefferson says, "This is indeed her time to shine. You're welcome to bid from the audience."

Small victories.

"Let's start the bidding at four hundred thousand." He initiates the bidding before I can tell him I need to start my music.

"No, that's not how this works." I toss my head back in frustration.

"Any lower and we're just wasting time. They have a show to get to." Jefferson's statement of fact doesn't help.

My brothers are messing everything up. Like always.

Hordes of leather-wearing bikers, complete with leather chaps, dome spike helmets, and beards, storm into the auction. What now?

Heat rises in my cheeks. Will I make Rebels'—my brothers' band—twenty thousand fans wait?

Jefferson must notice I'm trying to relax the tension in my shoulders. "Then again, what would it hurt to include everyone in the fun? Several of you were bidding on Bianca. Here's your chance to get back in the mix. Let's start Aurora where Bianca left off. Thirty thousand, do we—"

Several paddles fly into the air. The incoherent increases in dollar amount whiz past as my brothers drive it up. The higher the number, the longer it takes for anyone else to bid.

It's bittersweet to be partially responsible for such a huge donation at the expense of my dreams.

I'm sold.

To my stepbrothers.

I'll give them the designated four hours of help to get ready for Christmas, just as the auction advertised. And I'll hate them even more.

My little fantasy about losing my V-card to swanky billionaires will go die with all of my other crushed dreams.

Jack tosses me over his shoulder, but I beat my fists against his back.

"Calm down, Sis. Just having fun." His hands linger on my waist while I get my bearing on my heels.

Forcing myself to stop swooning at how his fingers wrap around me, I muster, "You're not the kind of fun I was hoping to have tonight."

"Ouch!" His smirk does things to me I can't control. My own body is betraying me.

"Time to go." Calvin interrupts our moment. Which is *not* a moment because he's my stepbrother.

I rush off the stage to grab my stuff and wish Cindy and Wendy well but Wendy is frantic and blurts out, "That motorcycle gang that came in…"

I nod.

"My stepbrothers are in it," Wendy says.

"You've got to be kidding me. Bianca's brothers, then mine, and now yours?"

We both turn to Cindy. "Any chance yours are showing up?"

"If I could only be so lucky." Cindy is more open about having a thing for her stepbrothers.

12

"Come on, Rory," Calvin calls loudly.

Damn him. "How many times have I said I'm done with that nickname?"

I hug my friends before my brothers cart me away. To do what? Watch their concert? Hang out in a corner with my V-card while they screw their groupies?

Great.

Three

Calvin

"What the hell was that?" I say from the driver's seat, my eyes meeting Aurora's in the rear-view mirror. She's sandwiched between Jack and Travis. I'm jealous.

"A fundraiser." Her sass makes me want to pull the car over and spank her.

"What exactly were you selling?" My eyes drift shamelessly downward and I thank the mirror for not letting me check out my stepsister's cleavage.

"My time." Her evasive answer makes my palms itch. A good smack on the ass would teach her... Hell, it would make my dick even harder. She's always been feisty. That's not likely to change, but it is likely to be fun.

Jack scoffs. "Christmas *Cherry* Auction. You do understand what was really being auctioned?"

She starts to answer, but Big D cuts her off. "And we won you fair and square."

With the help of the mirror, I shoot Big D a warning glance. The four of us had time on the ride over to clear up that we want her. In every way. But we're not discussing it with her until after the show.

"Don't remind me. I can already see the headline, the billionaire rockstars make a giant donation to the woman's shelter. Yay!" Irritation drips from her words. "You could have let me stay there with my friends."

"Not a chance." I can barely hold back from telling her our plan.

"Then take me home."

"We have a concert to get to. You did your good deed raising money for a charity. It's time for us to put on a show that pays the bills for a lot of hard-working people." Big D reaches between the seats and tries to take her hand, but she pulls away.

"You should have just stayed at your concert."

None of us has an answer. Should have...yes. But seeing her in that picture from backstage, before the auction, all four of us broke. I've never spoken to my brothers about my feelings for her, but I wasn't alone.

Did testosterone take over, to make us think we could convince her that we want her? Why is the one woman who doesn't swoon over us the one we're interested in?

We've always adored and protected her, but things are different now...seeing her as a grown woman. She still has our attention. She's fun and sparky. She's perfect.

Before I know it, my mind dives into the dark parts of my desire. I want her to be the mother of my children. *We* want to keep her knocked up.

And we have no idea how to get her to see us this way.

We had to get her off that stage because no one's going to fuck our little sister for money. I pull through the security gates to the private entrance.

"I still don't see why you're forcing me to watch your concert," she says as we walk quickly, guiding her inside.

"You're not watching the concert."

She stamps her foot down, halting our forward momentum, crosses her arms, and says, "You interrupted my fun evening with friends *and* you're not going to let me watch the concert? Great way to ruin a girl's evening!"

Oh, I want to ruin her, all right, but not in the way she's thinking.

"You're going to stay backstage," Jack says.

"I'm not staying backstage. I'll call an Uber."

She pulls her phone out of her purse.

"You're not going anywhere."

"Then the four hours I owe you start now. Oops, they started thirty minutes ago."

I hoist her over my shoulder and carry her to the meeting room where a member of our security team is stationed. I'm sure we had security in pursuit when we left unexpectedly, but this guy's in place.

16

Brian intercepts us as we put Aurora in the room. "We've been stalling, but they're running out of their best songs. You've got three minutes."

"You heard the man." Aurora makes a shooing motion. "You better get on stage."

God, I fucking love her sassiness. I want to resist just to get her worked up, but I holler over my shoulder to the bodyguard, "Nobody goes in or out except us."

"Tick tock," she says, "I'm only your hostage for three hours and twenty-nine more minutes."

Her dress shifted when I had her over my shoulder. Her tits are spilling out just a little bit more, A slight tug and I'd be able to see those tight little nipples. I physically turn my body toward the exit.

The bodyguard is staring at my chest. I look down. My black leather jacket and t-shirt are covered in glitter. I try to wipe it off, but my hands are covered, too.

She looks like a damn glitter factory exploded. She's always loved things that sparkle, and that's what I love about her. She sparkles, even without the messy addition.

I stride out of the room, Jack flanking me with Big D and Travis following. "We've got to forget about her until the show is over."

Jack laughs, "Tell your erection that."

Four

Aurora

The good news is that my brothers will be occupied for the next couple hours, running out the clock on the four hours I owe them.

I browse the room. The globe lights around the mirror and makeup on the counter indicate it's a dressing room, but the bulk of their stuff is somewhere else. It's kind of funny. My brothers have more makeup than me...except for glitter.

A set of Travis's drumsticks lay haphazardly on a couch next to hand written sheet music. I pick one page up. The words under the musical staff aren't English. He's into some weird stuff. He's the withdrawn, black hair hanging into his eyes, type—but on him, it's ridiculously sexy.

I've tried to keep my distance from my brothers, but the tabloids mentioned something about him tapping into the Viking roots of our family. I toss it aside.

Nobody knows what goes on in his head. He's probably as misunderstood as me. People wonder why I don't use their fame to catapult my career, but I don't share their dreams. I love theater, same as when they were younger, but I love working with kids. I work at the children's theater and want to run it someday.

Picking up a pair of Travis's drumsticks, I find they're heavier than I expected. Then again, they'd break if they weren't pretty sturdy. I try spinning the stick in my fingers, and it goes clattering to the floor. I try flipping it in the air and catching it, only to hit my head.

Fine, I'll give him credit for his show-off skills.

I look in the mirror. I'm the epitome of classic beauty: long blond hair, pale blue eyes, hourglass figure. Trailing a finger over my collarbone and down my chest, I wonder how my evening would have ended if my brothers hadn't intervened.

It should have been perfect. The Christmas Cherry Auction getting moved to the Aubergine Affair sex club made it a given that I would lose my V-card.

Were my brothers the only people who didn't get it? Or were they being the overprotective brothers they've always been? Will I ever shake free from being their little sister?

I lift one of my feet to a stool and start humming the classic stripper tune, slowly unzipping my boot. *I'm Sexy and I Know It* by LMFAO comes to mind.

I shift my weight to pull the boot off but lose my balance and almost twist my ankle. Thankfully, I fell against the countertop.

I zip my boot and return to the couch, trying to pronounce the weird words on Travis's music. Fail. Snapping a picture, I plan on finding a translation app.

For now, I'm done.

I head to the door, open it, and a thick arm shoots across the doorway, followed promptly by the bulk of the security guy, bodyguard, whatever he is.

"You're not going anywhere."

"I'm being held against my will." I try to lengthen my spine so that I come up somewhere higher than his armpits.

"Sorry, ma'am. I have orders to keep you here."

"Did you just ma'am me...Hudson?" I resort to the name on his lanyard when I fail to think of something clever.

"Yes, ma'am."

"You do realize I'm younger than you?"

"Yes ma'am."

Okay, that's not working. "I'm their sister."

"I'm aware of that, ma'am." He is the most polite, obnoxious person ever.

"My brothers don't have any right to keep me here."

"That's not for me to decide." He steps forward, leaving me no choice but to step back. When I'm clear of the door, he grabs it and pulls it shut, forcing me to my solitude.

Walking absent-mindedly around the room, I find bourbon under a t-shirt with Travis's stuff. I survey the rest of the room. Nothing else to drink.

Glancing at the closed door, I lift the bottle. "Thank you very much. I would love a drink."

I pour myself a shot and promptly down it. Wow! It's way smoother than the cheap stuff I've tried.

Pappy Van Winkle...what a silly name. But tasty. I bypass the glass and drink the last bit from the bottle. Were Travis's lips here? It didn't take long for the alcohol to start lowering my inhibitions. My fantasies refuse to be repressed any longer.

"Well, Pappy, maybe this doesn't have to be a terrible evening after all."

Pappy doesn't answer. I guess that's a good thing. If he does start talking back, I need to check myself.

"With a little more of your help, I might be able to convince my brothers to help me with the V-card issue." My brothers are sinfully gorgeous, experienced, and owe me for messing up my evening.

I grab my phone and add Wendy to a group chat with Bianca and Cindy then send a text: *I'm hidden backstage at my stepbrothers' concert. How is everyone else?*

It turns out Bianca's evening failed as badly as mine, and she has to address invitations for her stepmom first thing tomorrow. I offer to help. It'll give us time to swap stories.

The second shot must be taking hold because I'm considering a new, wild scenario. What if my brothers bought me because they know exactly what I was hoping for in that auction?

21

Five

Jack

I bolt off the stage and motion for Hudson to step away from the door. My brothers are still taking bows, but there's nothing I care about on that stage. Everything I want is behind this door.

I throw the door open and Aurora's holding an empty bourbon bottle to her mouth like a microphone, singing a slurred rendition of *All I Want for Christmas is You*. Her vocal talent is clear despite her drunkenness.

When she leans forward and points at me, my cock goes rock hard. I step closer and take the bottle from her hands.

"How much did you drink?"

"All of it."

"How much is all of it?"

"There was hardly anything left."

She walks her fingers up my chest and again sings the only line she seems to remember. It's a damn shame she's drunk, and my sister.

My brothers file in behind me, and Calvin demands, "What the fuck?"

Big D stops beside me. "Mind if I join in?"

Calvin steps to the other side. "She's drunk. What kind of men are you?"

"Her brothers." Travis overemphasizes the relation as he walks past us and flops on his chaise.

Yeah, but no. We're only related by our parents' marriage. Which should be enough to keep me from reacting the way I am.

"Jack's the..." Aurora giggles, and before I realize what she's doing, her delicate little fingers are on the crotch of my pants. No hiding how hard I am for her.

"The cocky one." She squeezes gently and I'm desperate to lose my morals, but my bad boy persona is a stage and publicity thing.

I cough at her unexpected move. She's bold and fun, but I've never seen this side of her. I've also never seen her drunk.

She says to Travis, "I read the tablets...tab...tabloids. I know exactly the kind of men you are."

"The tabloids don't know shit about the real us." Travis's head tips back.

"You're the tortured, broody one." She lolls her head toward Doug. "Big D's the playboy."

He catches her hand before she gropes him.

She pulls free and points toward Calvin. "And you, Mr. Bossy Pants…"

He cuts her off. "Yep. I'm the bossy one. I'm the oldest. I've always been responsible. Time to get you home."

"Not yet." She giggles while trying to appear defiant. "No sir, you're responsible so you owe me." She rambles about messing up her evening, overexplaining without explaining anything.

"What do we owe you?" Calvin taking her bait is a bit of a surprise.

"Everyone knows what the Christmas Cheery…Cheer…Cherry Auction is for, and you bought me. Now you have to fuck me."

Bam! She said it. The thought that's haunted me from the moment I heard she was in the auction. She was in it for sex. My chest tightens. My fists ball. If we hadn't bought her…

Travis, for the first time ever, moves fast and is at Aurora's side. "That's not how this works. We won four hours of your time, and apparently you're going to need to use four hours to sleep this off."

"But—"

"You're in no condition to do anything but sleep it off."

"You're not the boss of me. You can't do this."

"Come on." I try to help her to the door, but she slaps at me.

"You should have stayed here and blabbed along to music that's so loud no one can hear your crappy lyrics. We could have all had a good night."

"You don't mean that."

"You ruined my night. You owe me. You're always screwing things up. I hate you."

She's kind of cute-drunk, but her words, albeit impaired, sting. Is there something to them? She wouldn't say that if she was sober, would she?

"We'll take you home, let you sleep it off." Travis's eternally dark and broody expression makes him hard to read.

Calvin adds, "We're taking her back to our place. Make sure she doesn't get into trouble."

"It's now or never, Pappy. I have to help my friend address invitations in the morning."

My balls threaten to blow a load at her calling Calvin Pappy. Jealousy? I'm totally fucked, in the wrong way.

"We'll take you wherever you need to be in the morning." Calvin's stoic response dismisses the nickname, but I'm stuck.

What if the truth in her earlier statement is that she wants to fuck us? I can't let that go. "We'll drop you off in the morning, but when you're done, you have some explaining to do."

Six

Aurora

Putting the last zip code on the final envelope for Bianca's stepmom's invitations, I sit back and relax. "I can't believe we finished all thousand invites."

Cindy came, too, which was a huge help.

Bianca says, "Thank you so much. I wouldn't have been able to enjoy my brothers last night if I had to do these all on my own."

I'm truly happy for her. Even though she didn't have sex, she had a lot of fun. Cindy did, too. And rumors are swirling about Wendy's brothers clearing out the sex club for time with her, but she hasn't messaged us yet. Even though the guys took me home to change clothes, I brush stray glitter off an envelope. "Three out of four isn't bad."

An uncomfortable silence is met with sympathetic smiles. I've killed the mood. "It's fine. My brothers are going to get an earful when they pick me up. They want to talk about last night."

Cindy pats my hand. "They may just be worried about image, like my brothers. Their night with me has to stay super-secret. They're already in trouble with their coach for a rowdy weekend. Their huge bid last night is all they can afford the media to publicize. The fun side of being a celebrity is great until something goes wrong and then the public scrutiny is vicious."

"I can't imagine living like that." A great reminder that shacking up with my stepbrothers has drawbacks. Our parents already can't separate stage persona from real life. It's been a sore point for years.

Bianca puts the pens away and grabs my hand. "You're bound to find out someday, Aurora. You're so talented. Have you heard back from the *Mama Mia* audition?"

"The director lost interest in me when he found out my brothers will be out of town." Such is my fate. My brothers interfere even when they don't do anything.

Bianca organizes the invitations in a box to take to the post office. "I'm sorry, sweetie."

Cindy asks, "Are you still auditioning for *Wicked*?"

"I'm going to focus on theater management, getting my foot in the door at the children's theater. People should be less worried about whether I bring famous brothers to the table."

Cindy gives me a hug. "Your time will come."

"You'll be brilliant whether you're on stage or managing it." Bianca toys with another piece of my glitter that's stuck to an envelope. "I better get these to the post office before my evil stepmother sees that you added your personal sparkle."

"My brothers are waiting for me."

"Consider the audition, though," Bianca encourages me as we head to the elevator. "Having a big role like that under your belt can't hurt."

"You're right. Why punish myself? I want that role." Perhaps this director won't ask if my brothers will attend a performance. And so what if they do? Being cast in a big role will only help my ultimate dream of running a theater. I pull out my phone and reply to the email confirming my audition time.

The elevator ride down from the penthouse gives me time to consider the immediate topic. My brothers. Rather than give them an earful about ruining my night, I'll get a rideshare to take me to my car. I don't owe them anything.

Seven

Travis

Our tour bus pulls up to the building where Aurora was helping her friend and I motion for my brothers to stay put. "I'll get her."

I crave a few seconds alone with her. Taking the steps out of the bus, the sparkle on my boots catches my attention. If only I could explain that she permeates my soul the way her glitter left its mark on everything.

My brothers and I had the most bizarre but honest conversation of our lives. We all want Aurora, even if it means sharing her. We live together, work together, play together, and we want Aurora to be a part of that, at any cost. We're not naïve. The public will be cruel.

It's one of many things weighing on our minds.

Calvin's on the phone with our tour manager discussing our potential world tour. I'm undecided on it. My Viking roots are calling to me and a world tour would mean less time to develop the concept. It would also mean we're even farther from Aurora.

She's exiting the elevator, pointing past me as I enter the lobby.

"The tour bus? Really?"

Her friends give her a hug, whisper something, and she waves for them to leave.

"Hello, Aurora. It's good to see you too." I don't mean it as sarcastic as it comes out.

"Why are you in the tour bus?"

"We're on tour. It's the only way we'll have time alone with you."

"What is that supposed to mean? We fit in the SUV last night. Where is it?"

"One of the stagehands is driving it. We have a show an hour away."

"I'm not getting on the tour bus."

"Why not?" I try to take her hand, but she shrugs away.

"Because I have things to do."

"We need to talk about last night."

"I'll spare your vocal cords the lecture. You didn't like my behavior. Thank you for taking care of me. You're such great big brothers. I'll get a ride back to my car." She's fucking sassing me.

I love it and hate it all at the same time. I crave her closeness. I crave her enthusiasm. I crave being able to sort out my very confusing feelings for her.

Shoving all of that aside, I strategize how to get her on the bus.

"We should have asked if you could spend a few days with us instead of just showing up in the bus."

"I have an audition, and I have a job."

"Do you have work today?"

Her bravado vanishes. "No."

"I'll help you run lines. And I promise, we aren't going to lecture you about last night. We have a proposition for you based on something you said. And if you object, we'll get you back for your audition."

"Promise?"

"I'd never lie to you."

With hesitation, she makes her way to the bus. She sits in the seat closest to the door and I take one opposite her. I drum my thumbs on the arm of my chair. It's my nerves. I don't know how we're going to explain this. That we want her.

Now that she's sober, it could go over like a lead balloon.

"What's that you're humming?" she asks.

I didn't realize I had been. Was I actually loud enough to be heard over the road noise of the bus? I get too lost in my head sometimes. Most of the time.

"It's a Viking chant I'm working on."

Big D pipes in. "Yeah, doing his broody, melancholic Viking shit. It all sounds like either a death march or a war chant."

31

Calvin is quick to add, "It's something he's doing on the side. The band is still going strong. Making bank."

"Is that why I'm here? So you can tell me how popular you are?" She glares at me.

"No, we want to get to know you better," Big D says.

"Okay, then you need to know that I have an audition. A job. A life. I'm more than just your little sister."

"What are you auditioning for?"

She sighs. "I shouldn't tell you because you'll interfere, but you could ask around and find out anyway. *Wicked*."

"That's awesome. But why not take our help?" Big D asks.

"If you show up, everyone will think I got the role because of you. Please don't mess this up for me. I truly love theater, and I can't enjoy it if all of the focus is on you. I just want to trust that I have what it takes."

She doesn't have to explain to me that she's all grown up. I lean forward. "We didn't realize we were causing problems when we came to your shows. We can change. We can give you your own space. You're an adult. Trust me, we know that. And if any of us hadn't realized it, we did at the auction last night."

"Then why didn't you leave me alone, let me do the auction my way?"

The words catch in my throat. Now would be a great time for some bourbon. I force the words out. "If someone had bought you last night, would you have had sex with them?"

"That's none of your business." I toy with the sash around my waist, giving far too much attention to the white snowflakes set against the blue satin.

Jack says, "I beg to differ since you grabbed my crotch and said we needed to fuck you."

She shrinks back. "Did I do that?"

"Even gave a little squeeze." Jack raises his eyebrows at me.

Now that we're solidly into the topic of last night, I'm nervous about seeing what she'll admit to.

"What the fuck! You're not auditioning for *Wicked*." Has Calvin listened to anything that was just said?

I cringe at the photo as he holds his phone up. My brothers and I did a lot of theater growing up, even as we formed the band. If our music hadn't taken off, we'd still be doing theater. We all love putting on a show. But not for the slave driver who's running *Wicked*.

She throws her hands up. "I told you about the audition two minutes ago. And I expressly said I didn't want you to interfere. Did you listen to anything I said?"

She waves her hands in front of her bowed head.

I've never wanted to punch Calvin more than at this moment.

Aurora stands up. "No, this isn't happening. You don't get to parent me. We have parents and their lack of appreciation for the arts is bad enough. This is my decision. Stay out of it."

Eight

Jack

We've put Aurora on the defensive, which is exactly wrong. I move closer to her, sit on the table, and block her view of Calvin.

She waves me off. "And to think I wanted to... Don't you have groupies to impress? I shouldn't have agreed to get on the bus."

"We're just trying to help," Calvin says as his phone rings and he excuses himself to go to the back room of the bus.

"You guys have career blocked me. You've cock blocked me."

"Whoa!" I put a hand on her shoulder. "We've cock blocked you?"

"Well, in a way. It's the same thing as careers. Either people love me or hate me because I'm your sister. I love acting, the pure art of it, and want to do it with people who share my passion. I don't want to be asked if my brother could do a promo spot for a show or if one of my brothers would be interested in a double date. I'm never seen for me."

Travis is taken aback. "Sorry, Aurora, I had no idea. But I hear you about following your passion with like-minded individuals.

That's why I'm looking into the Viking stuff regardless of what The Rebels fans think."

Big D offers a sympathetic approach. "Look, there are good and bad directors in the theater world, like every profession. The wrong one can be a miserable experience. We spent our time vying for audition spots and taking whatever was thrown our way. Even when our band started taking off, some of our managers made us miserable. You've got to be careful with these people. Calvin was just trying to point out that we have experience. We know that director is bad news."

Aurora seems to listen when he mentions our struggles. She was probably more aware of our successes, not our failures.

"Yeah," I say, "It's hard to make your dreams come true. Taking on stage personas is how we hang onto our love of acting."

"So with your spectacular acting skills, you chose to be cocky?" A lightness shines through her tone.

"Us? You were the one grabbing crotches last night. Haven't you heard of consent?" I chuck her under the chin.

She purses her lips. "Sorry. I know it's not a good excuse, but the bourbon may have given me too much courage."

"You're forgiven. Now, we've made your life miserable, so as you said, we owe you."

"You can't control other people's obsession with you. Just no more jumping in to save the day, unless I ask."

We all voice agreement.

"But there is one more thing you mentioned last night that we'd like to explore."

Nervous excitement flips through her eyes. "Could we just forget about last night?"

"Sweet Aurora, your sassy little mouth said something last night that I'll never be able to forget."

Her eyes fall shut and her breaths quicken. She grins sheepishly. "Remember the bourbon."

"You mean Pappy? And how you said it to Calvin?"

"Does he hate me for that?" Her hands cover her mouth.

I slide onto the arm of her chair and pull her hands from her mouth, allowing my finger to skim over her lips. "He'll have to speak for himself, but it made the rest of us jealous."

"Jealous?" She licks where my finger touched.

"Not only did you torment us with that nickname, but you said we had to fuck you."

Did all of us stop breathing? Road noise fills the void. Everything hinges on her response.

Big D breaks the silence from across the table. "Is that what you were hoping for at the auction?"

Travis adds, "You can be honest. Look how much clarity we're getting now that we're opening up to each other."

She nods but turns her gaze to her fingers, fiddling with the ribbon around her dress.

"So you were hoping that whoever bought you would be worthy?"

"Something like that."

"A *Pappy*?"

She laughs. "Please don't ever remind me that I used that term."

"But it was—"

"No." She shakes her head. "Can't go there with my brothers."

I step in front of her and extend my arms. "Can you go here?"

Her brow furrows, but she nods.

I scoop her into my arms and carry her to the couch. Her long, golden hair fans around her as I lay her on her back.

"If..." I emphasize the word, "the winner was worthy, would you have wanted him to take you missionary style?"

Our eyes lock and I swear I can see my future. The sparkle in her eyes returns, so I swing a leg over her, pinning her beneath me.

"Would you have wanted him to crawl on top of you and make slow, sweet love?" I lower my hips.

Her answer is barely a whisper. "Yes."

"Or maybe you'd prefer this." I hoist her up and she squeals, clinging to me. Her embrace is too good to pass up, but I'm running with my plan. Flipping her over, I settle her on all fours, grip one hand around her hip to hold her up, and press my other hand on her back, forcing her shoulder down. My strained erection presses into her winter version of a sundress, and I resist the temptation to get her skirt out of the way even though I'm still clothed. "Being ridden hard and deep from behind."

Travis kneels, lowering his lips to her ear. "So what is it?"

"I don't know."

My cock throbs inside my jeans. Good enough. With her holding the position, I release my grip and inch her skirt up. "Say the word and I can make you sing the praises of all things holy."

Big D positions himself against the wall next to us. "It's your call, Aurora. You pick the position. You pick the man. We're here to please you."

Pulling her body upward, I rotate her to sit across my lap. I kiss her hair then tuck it behind her ear and nibble. My other hand rests on her thigh, my fingertips inching closer to her pussy. "Anything you want, just know that I'd love to get my mouth on your pussy. Make sure you're good and ready for a cock. Whatever you prefer."

A beat passes before she says, "I don't know."

Big D, Travis, and I divert our eyes from her to each other.

I consider the possibility that's weighed on me. The true struggle I had with her taking part in the cherry auction. "Have you ever had sex?"

"I haven't."

"So the whole cherry auction thing was for real?" Big D fails to hide his excitement.

Her shoulders hunch up. "If I didn't feel a connection, I could have just done four hours of cleaning or holiday prep. That was for real."

"But if you did connect?" I wrap my arms around her waist.

The blush that takes over her cheeks is brighter than any of the sparkly makeup she wears. She looks at me from under her eyelashes. "You said to be honest, right?"

"Always."

"I was hoping to lose my V-card."

"And you were mad at us for ruining your plan?"

She nods.

"People say we're the naughty ones." Big D's grin is about to split his face in half.

I hold back my frustration that she was willing to have her first time with a stranger. Crisis averted, as I hold her in my arms. My possessive streak soars way beyond big brother protectiveness. She's mine. In every way. And I intend to prove it.

Nine

Aurora

Jack's steel rod of a cock is underneath me. Did he already know I was a virgin? It doesn't matter.

The big question is, did the bourbon kill too many of my brain cells? I've all but admitted that I've had a crush on the very brothers who've annoyed me for so many years. Am I willing to choose them for my first time?

Them?

How do I pick one? They way the three of them are surrounding me has me feeling like sex on a swivel. Maybe I channeled Marilyn all too well. I recall the movie excerpt where all of the men are clamoring for her. She's the center of attention.

Jack's arms tighten around me as he nuzzles his head against mine.

Is that what I want? All of them? Nobody said anything about one. What about all four?

Jack tucks a finger under my chin, pulling my attention from the door Calvin is behind. Our lips are mere inches apart.

"I could help you figure out the answers to those questions."

"*We* could," Big D is quick to point out, stroking his stubble. Is he imagining us together?

"We're all here for you, Aurora, even Calvin. See what it's like to be loved by all of us."

"Is that the way you do it with groupies?"

Jack's breathing deepens. I might've missed it if I wasn't sitting on his lap.

If I'm going to bare my secrets, so are they, although their sexual habits are more public than mine. "You said we should be honest."

"We've never shared a woman," Jack clarifies.

Travis is tense. "People spread rumors. You were backstage. Did you see any women?"

"I figured it was just because you had me back there."

"That's how it is every time." Travis is painfully clear.

"So why me?"

"It's just something we know."

Big D leans in. "Let me kiss you."

I nod. My tongue darts over my lips. This is real. I lean forward and close my eyes.

He cups my neck and his lips fall softly on my cheek before he rests his head against mine.

My cheek? My eyes flit open. He's holding me so tenderly I don't want it to end. I close them again and sink into his touch. We simply exist for what feels like an eternity before he pulls away.

My lips part, hopeful for more as he angles his head. Our lips meet. He accepts my offer for more than a chaste kiss. The passion. The acceptance. They're everything I dreamed of.

I could lose myself in this forever.

He pulls away, resting his forehead against mine. "We want to make you happy. Go on tour with us. You'll be the highlight of everything we do."

How can a kiss make me want to re-evaluate everything? My factual answer is half-hearted. "My audition is on Monday."

"If it's that important, we'll get you back in time. Let us worship you until then." Travis's smile is forced.

"But consider who you'd be—"

I put a finger to Jack's lips. "Shh. No talking me out of it."

Doug reaches up and angles one of the lights on me, then reaches to the side and does the same with two more. "If it's the spotlight you want, we'll put you in it."

"I don't need fame."

"But you do need answers. Ready for your first lesson so you can make an educated decision?" Jack winks.

"As long as you promise."

He places a finger on my lips. "We promise to get you back to your audition if you insist on going."

Doug takes my hand. "Are you sure you're okay with this? All of us?"

"How could I refuse? You're every girl's dream."

"Are we your dream?" Travis is sweet to clarify, but does it really matter? He's not typically the guy who needs his ego stroked.

"We're being honest with each other," Big D reminds me.

I nod.

"Lesson number one, continued from last night." Jack repositions me on his lap, spreading my legs over his thighs. Shoving my skirt out of the way, he takes my hand and presses it against the front of his pants. "You remember how hard you make me, Baby?"

As if I'd need a reminder. Playing up my innocence, I ask, "Has it been this hard the whole time?"

Jack's mouth goes slack. "In the interest of honesty, I took an extra-long shower and jacked myself off thinking about you."

I flash a teasing smile. "I was joking. But thanks for the honesty."

He shakes his head. "Guys, anyone else willing to admit how badly they need Aurora?"

"I wrote a song about her," Travis says. "Then I imagined making slow, sweet love to you under the stars."

"So yeah, he jacked off too." Jack shifts his attention to Big D.

"Winning you in the auction left me in a world of hurt...every hour on the hour."

"Impressive." I wonder if he's joking.

"Enough about us. Why don't you get her zipper, Travis."

In a combined effort, my dress is unzipped, pulled out from under my bottom, and slipped over my head. Jack rubs his finger over my bra. My sensitive nipples tingle like never before. My sex aches, and I'm pretty sure I'm so wet, Jack's pants will be soaked.

"I'm not sure what to do."

"Enjoy being in the spotlight while we get to know you better." Jack drops one hand between my legs. His finger teases over the damp silky fabric, giving him the most wicked smile I have ever seen.

My breaths fall in sync with the movement of his fingers. My body takes on a mind of its own, bucking and tightening as he reads my every reaction.

Doug tilts my face to the side and locks lips with me. His tongue explores my mouth. I love getting attention from both of them. I love the spotlight more than I thought.

Travis is watching from the side. Then I think it's his hand that slides onto my thigh, works up my waist, over my back. I think he's the one who tucks hair behind my ear, but I'm losing track.

Kisses are harder to cling to as Jack's fingers move inside my panties to massage my clit, taking me to the edge. I'm about to lose control. The whimpering is coming from deep within me.

Doug's hand is cupped behind my head, holding me close through all of my gasps and moans.

The orgasm crescendos so huge inside of me it's an explosion of energy. My body shakes as my brothers carry me through blissful oblivion, my conscious remnants drifting until I finally settle back into the moment.

They've each eased their touches. Doug rests his cheek against mine, still cradling my head in the nook between his neck and shoulder. Travis's fingers trail lazily over my back. Jack mutters, "I love—"

"What the hell?" Calvin came back.

My arms cross reflexively, hiding my chest as if we've done something wrong. Have we? And was Jack about to say that he loves me?

Ten

Calvin

Hanging up with the tour manager, I'm undecided about the proposed schedule. Rory has changed everything. I'm the brother who can find the logic and stay level-headed through anything, but now...she's clouding my judgment.

What does that mean for my gut- and heart-driven brothers?

And what would an intimate relationship do to our already broken relationship with our parents? They think my brothers and I are depraved because of our stage personas and they think she's destined to poverty because she's more concerned with the art of acting than money.

I call them, as I always do when we return to our hometown.

It goes straight to voicemail, as always.

I keep my message short. They won't respond. They never do.

"Hi, Mom and Dad. We're back in the area. Would love to see you over Christmas. Our manager's trying to convince us to do a world tour. Maybe you have insight on cities we should—"

A cry from the other room stops me cold. Shit! I hit the End Call button. Is Rory having an orgasm?

Throwing the door open, I'm paralyzed as I watch my three brothers make Aurora come. What happened after I left the room? Weren't we trying to convince her not to audition for that prick?

"Our sister's a pro at having orgasms. I've never heard anything like it." Big D tries to calm me. "Turns out sis hasn't had sex."

How far did they go? Jealousy, irritation, and desire have a battle of the bands inside of me. "I'm in there working, and you're..."

I've scared Rory. Shit. I stop myself. Breathe.

"Relax man, it's not like you didn't know we all wanted her," Jack says.

I shove Doug out of the way and caress Rory's bare shoulder. "I didn't mean to scare you."

She smiles but doesn't relax her arms.

They started without me. I was working and they decided to play. They had their hands on her while I was sending a message to our parents. I kick all of the thoughts from my mind and focus.

"You're a virgin?" I make a mental note that my brothers still have their pants on, and am eager to hear the answer from her sweet lips.

"I am, but they said you're all willing to teach me. That you'd be okay with this."

"I am." I point at my brothers. "And if you had waited until I was available, I wouldn't have recorded our sister's orgasm in a message to Mom and Dad."

"You recorded it?" Her eyes widen.

"I hung up as fast as I could. Hopefully the receiver didn't pick it up clearly."

"Can you unsend the message?" Aurora asks.

Shaking my head, I say, "It was a voicemail."

Big D offers a sad truth. "They'll probably think it's just some groupie in the background. They think all we do is have sex between concerts. That's what everybody thinks we do, but it pays the bills, so it's all good."

"It's not all good. This..." Rory motions to all of us, climbs off Jack's lap, and reaches for her dress. "We shouldn't be doing this."

"I think we did it quite well," Jack says.

"But look how close this came to a huge mistake. When we get to your hotel, I'll get a ride home and focus on my audition."

I clamp my hands around hers, holding the balled-up dress to her chest. "Slow down. I'm not about to be the only brother who didn't get a taste of you."

She sputters. "Um, well...no one *tasted* me. We were just getting started on some sex lessons."

"Good, then you still need a teacher."

She glances at each brother. No one objects.

"No one has to know. Consider them private lessons." It's unlikely I can keep that promise, and it pains me to even remotely lie to her. But for now, it's the truth. Gently tugging the dress, I'm able to slip it from her hands.

I had no idea a woman could be so perfect.

Jack stands behind her, slides his hands from her shoulders to her fingertips, then laces their hands together and moves them onto her belly.

Damn if my mind doesn't go straight to thoughts of her being full of my baby. She'd make the perfect mother. Is that what Jack's thinking too?

He moves their hands upward, caressing her breasts, going up to her neck into her hair. It's a tease. He's making her caress herself for me.

"You know you want her, Calvin. Teach this goddess how good your mouth will feel on her pussy."

I rake my hand through my hair, then let my gaze linger on her long eyelashes, the pale blue of her eyes, the look of hopefulness.

"Has anyone ever gone down on you, Sweetheart?" The possibility of going to Hell for putting my mouth on my stepsister's pussy isn't enough to stop me from dropping to my knees.

Everything blurs as her scent intoxicates me. I tease my thumb over her hot, wet, pink silky panties. "They've already got you wet. You smell so good, you're going to ruin me."

"I don't want to ruin you." Her fingers drag through my hair, ensuring my ruin.

I cup my hands in that sweet spot where her ass meets the top of her thigh. She's mine.

"Hold her," I say as I dive in.

Jack wraps his arms around her and lifts so I can strip her panties down.

But he doesn't set her down. He works his hands under her. The other brothers, on either side, each take one of her legs and splay her wide for me.

Holy fuck, I am definitely going to Hell. I kiss, then lick, then suck on her pretty, pink, untouched pussy. Her juices are the ambrosia to the gods. The buck of her hips ensures she's enjoying the lesson.

Being between her legs makes me feel like a god. And then she comes undone.

The world could cease to exist and I wouldn't care. I've claimed my sister.

Eleven

Jack

Heading into the last verse of our encore, Big D gives us a nod, letting us know that he'll take the improv before the last note. He segues into his solo, fingers flying over the keyboard, and my thoughts drift to earlier when I was holding Aurora against my body, Travis and Big D held her legs, and Calvin sank to his knees in front of her.

Each shake and whimper of her orgasm is ingrained in my soul.

Staying engaged with the audience is important, but not today. I turn my attention to the side of the stage where she's waiting. Did she hear me say that I love her before Calvin walked in on us?

She hasn't brought it up, but she also didn't go home. She signed up for more lessons and we've had one hell of a day with her.

It's still not enough. Until she commits to being ours, I fear she'll consider us temporary.

Can she see me as Jack, a guy who's completely enamored with her, and willing to throw everything away to claim her? Or does she just want Jack, the bad boy of The Rebels? Will letting down my façade help us grow closer, or drive her away?

Big D's going crazy on the keyboard, his signature move of turning around backward and still playing something that makes a little bit of musical sense.

I work my way to the side of the stage. Calvin's watching me, no doubt wondering what I'm up to. Slipping my bass strap from around my neck, I split my attention between Big D and Aurora.

When he gives the final nod, I bang out my cord, set my bass out of the way, and rush to Aurora.

"Aren't you supposed to stay out there?" She looks over my shoulder.

I lace my fingers with hers, bringing them up to her shoulders, and pin her against the wall.

"Show's over. Time to focus on the only thing that's been on my mind."

"Don't be silly."

I rock my hips into her. "Does that feel silly?"

She shakes her head. Even if she'd verbalized an answer, I wouldn't have been able to hear. The crowd's going wild. It was a high-energy performance. I'd wondered if the energy was from the crowd or just from me, knowing that Aurora was waiting for me, for us.

"I love you, Aurora." I lowered my mouth to her ear. "I need to make love to you."

Her response is hard to hear above the noise. "Is that my next lesson, make love? It sounds so polite. I thought you were supposed to be the bad boy."

My chest tightens. I won't force her to acknowledge my first statement. "I'll be whatever you want me to be."

Glancing over my shoulder, I confirm that the audience can't see us. Then I unleash my desire. Gripping her chin, turning her face to mine, I lock my lips on hers, channeling that bad boy energy.

"You want a bad boy, then you're going to get fucked right here." I need to get my dick inside of her. I need to make her scream. I need to make her feel good. I need to make her mine.

"Let me fuck you bare, Aurora." I lower a hand, shove her dress between her legs, and cup her sex without applying pressure.

She trails kisses over my shoulder.

"You have to consent."

Her hips are wiggling against my hand and she whimpers. "You have my consent, always and forever."

Pulling some petty sibling shit like 'no take-backs' would kill the bad boy vibe. I damn sure hope she meant it.

I'm about to be her first. I'm energized with how right this feels. With the energy of the crowd still screaming. Our brothers are feeding the applause, playing extra little riffs.

We work together to get her skirt up and her panties down.

"We're going to get caught." Her excitement over it surprises me.

"You like that, don't you? The thrill of the risk?" I lift her and press my tip against her wet pussy.

"Our brothers are going to be pissed." Her breaths come even faster and her cheeks flush.

"You're a naughty girl, trying to get me in trouble." I lock my eyes on hers and tilt my hips, forcing her virgin lips to spread for me.

She gasps, her expression pinches, then softens happily.

The rush is intense. I force myself to stop. "You okay? I'll be gentle."

"I want my first time to be memorable." She hooks her legs around me. "I want you to fuck me like we're about to get in trouble."

"I don't want to do that with you, Aurora, not for your first time."

She rocks her hips hard and fast against me. "Hurry, they're going to catch us."

Shit! My balls are ready to unload per her request, but I don't let them. Leaning into her, I pin her firmly against the wall. "If I'm going hard and fast, you have to keep your eyes open. I have to see that you're okay."

The amount of certainty in her baby blues is staggering. Where did my sister learn that? I fuck her as hard as I can, pounding her into the wall. Every sensation grows more intense. Louder. Clearer. The earth shakes underneath us.

Except that it really does, or at least the stage does. And the roar of the crowd is too close.

The clench of Aurora's pussy around my shaft snaps me back to a solitary focus—making her come.

Her fingernails dig into my shoulder as she cries out and falls limp against me. I don't want this to end, but something's wrong. Sharp commands from our security team direct us to leave the stage.

The audience must be out of control. This can't be happening. The only fuck my balls give is the one that involves Aurora. They pump surge after surge of my seed into her.

I lean to the side while my hips insist on finishing their primal function. The crowd is rushing the stage.

Bodyguards and security are in place, pushing them back, but there are too many audience members on stage to count.

If I can see them, they can see us. Fuck!

Some of them have their phones held high. This will be public soon.

Calvin's rounding the corner and Big D is right behind him. They look horrified when they see me pinning Aurora to the wall.

Twelve

Big D

What the hell? We're having an emergency and Jack's over here fucking Aurora?

Security personnel don't bat an eye, just add Jack carrying Aurora as they usher us backstage. There's too much chaos to stop.

Safely inside the tour bus, we all turn to Jack, who's set Aurora on the couch and is just now putting his dick back in his pants. That couldn't have been a comfortable run to safety.

The bus is in motion, carrying us away with a police escort. We're all supercharged with adrenaline, except Aurora. She's blissed out.

Rather than yell at Jack for claiming her without talking to the rest of us, I sit beside her and lean her body against mine. "Can I make you mine?"

My question perks her up. "Can I get on your lap to do it?"

"Sure thing. I'm just here to make you happy."

I've barely got my pants shoved to mid-thigh when she straddles me and drags her fingernails over my erection. It's an electric surge. Pre-cum spurts out and she swirls her fingers through it.

"Big D... I guess your name isn't just because you don't like being called Doug."

"I'll sure as hell take that compliment." I catch my brothers taking a look, but nothing comes of it since Aurora's ready.

Her hands are on my shoulders and my hands are around her waist.

"You want to lead the pace?" I ask.

Her mouth opens to answer but she interrupts her own response by teasing herself on my rock-hard cock. Wiggling her hips back and forth, she combines our wetness before sinking onto me.

The start-and-stop of her motion is sweet torture. Her warmth and tightness welcome me. I throb inside of her, barely holding off an orgasm.

She picks up the pace, her head lolls back, and I quietly nod and ask Calvin to strip her dress off of her while she's pleasing herself at my expense.

I'm not complaining. My little stepsister sure loves fucking as much as I do.

Calvin strips her bare, and her tits bounce in my face. I lean forward, catching her nipple with my tongue. It makes her shiver, which makes her pussy clench, which makes my dick twitch. Yeah, it's a hell of a chain reaction until her pussy doesn't stop clenching. Over and over again, she constricts around me.

I have to take over, pumping her on my cock as she loses her ability to focus. She comes so hard, she obliterates the road noise of the highway.

"I love you." And I'm helpless to resist. I shoot rope after rope of cum into her womb. Baby-making time. I'm a bastard for wanting that. We all are.

When I regain my composure, I slide her off of my cock, turning her sideways on my lap, and cradle her against me. "You better rest. From what I saw, you took it pretty hard with Jack, and you didn't go easy on yourself with me."

Of course, Travis and Calvin might disagree, but they nod understanding.

I hate that I'll have to let her go at some point, but I hold on for now. Much like I hold on to the hope of getting her pregnant. She's bound to hit me with a wrecking ball at any moment and say that she's on birth control. For now... Hope breeds eternal...or something like that.

Travis disappears for a second, then comes back with a washcloth. He sits at her feet, rests his hand on her knees. "Let me clean you up."

He eases her legs apart, then tenderly cares for her with the washcloth. The warm water drips on me and it feels damn good, but I know better than to ask him to clean me up. Even if Aurora was offering, I wouldn't want her to. I want to bask in her scent for eternity.

He's paying a little too much attention, so I tell him, "Fuck off. Let her rest."

She falls asleep in my arms. It's the sweetest thing that's ever happened. I'm usually up for a rowdy, good time, but it turns out this tops everything. Might mean I actually have a tender side.

And the way my heart feels, I think I'm getting set up for the biggest adventure of my life. I kiss Aurora on the head as she stirs. "Sorry, I didn't mean to wake you."

"I wasn't really sleeping."

"You need to travel with us. We can have this all the time. You can travel the world with us."

Calvin says, "If we do the world tour. If not, just stay with us."

She squirms to sit upright against me. "If I get the part, I'll have rehearsals. I can't be on the road." She lays out the plan, the rehearsal schedule, and the performance dates. "In fact, I should do some vocal work." She pushes off of me and walks toward the back of the tour bus.

But Travis, drumsticks in hand, swings them around her waist and locks her in with his other hand. "Take a break. Just for today."

Thirteen

Aurora

Why do I love him forcing me to stop? Why am I so turned on by being restrained?

The drumsticks pressed low across my belly and hip bones... I like resisting against them. As I try to step farther, he pulls tighter.

"Where are you going? Don't let our talk about tours make you think you have to practice," he says with his arms wrapped around me.

I want him to restrain me more, and in different ways. I wrap my hands around the drumsticks. Over my shoulder, I say, "Can I see these?"

"Sure." He lets me take the sticks. I spin around and kiss the ends of them.

"You want them back?" The tour bus is big, but only so big, so I don't have much of a plan to run away with them. But we're near the front and I want to be chased.

His eyes narrow. "You can keep them."

I drag the drumsticks down my neck, through my cleavage, and stop on my belly. "Are you sure you don't want them?" I step away tauntingly.

"On second thought..." He steps closer, eyeing me questioningly.

I scurry a few feet toward the back of the bus, but he catches me before I get to the door that I had hoped to be able to try to close between us.

His arms wrap around me. The security that washes over me is so wrong. I shouldn't want any of this. But I do. And I'm going to accept it.

He takes the sticks from my hands and he presses them between my legs. The angle he has them at catches my clit, causing me to shudder. I squirm away but he catches me from behind, grips my wrist firmly, turning me into his chest, and pinning both of my hands behind me. His huge paw is able to grip both of my wrists and the drumsticks.

"Are you taunting me?"

"Are you going to punish me?" I bat my eyelashes at him, hoping he'll continue with our little game. He strides forward, forcing me back until we pass through the doorway.

He turns me, backing me against a desk. "Maybe it's not so bad Calvin insisted on having this in the bus."

I glance over my shoulder, and thankfully the top is clear.

He leans me back, then holds both of my hands in front of my stomach with one hand while he unzips his pants with the other. He helps me get my feet onto the desk, which is much more comfortable than when my legs were dangling.

Then he leans into my legs and fucks me hard. A hint of light enters his dark eyes as we drive each other to climax.

Fourteen

Travis

My heart fails to beat as my brothers and I pile into the SUV in a mad dash to get to Aurora's audition. We want to celebrate with her afterward, even though she won't be notified right away. We know she deserves the part.

The question is if she wants us there. It's the thing keeping all of us silent as Calvin drives.

I was pissed when we woke up in the hotel this morning and she'd snuck out. I've never had sex so good it left me basically unconscious.

She left a cute little note with hearts on it saying she didn't want to bother us.

We'd promised to get her to the audition, but apparently she had a friend come pick her up. My lungs barely take air. She had to plan ahead to leave us.

The drive gives me time to get lost in the memory of making love to her. She liked being controlled. She liked being restrained. I'm not nearly done exploring that.

I rub my hand over my mouth. Her lingering scent serves as a reminder of what we've done.

She's a sexual goddess beast. That may not have been a thing before, but now, it's alive and well in Aurora.

My chest has phantom vibrations as I recall our second round of sex. She wanted my hand over her mouth to keep her from making too much noise in the hotel room. Her head thrashing side to side made it extra fun. She had me throw her on the bed, something she'd seen in a movie. Then she wanted me to force her to stay before she could get up. She really gets off on being controlled.

My cock nearly splits through the leather of my pants, it swells so hard and fast. I wonder if she'll be up for some CNC, if she's even heard of consensual non-consent. Would that push a limit? I'd sure as fuck like to find out.

I'll talk to her after the celebration. *Celebration*...that's fucked. I'm ecstatic that she's pursuing her dreams, but they're in conflict with our schedule. We have obligations to a lot of workers that support us. We'd be nothing without them.

But I'm nothing without Aurora.

We keep rockstar personas in public, but we're businessmen behind the scenes. None of that will be helped by shacking up with our sister. More fucking conflict.

I think we're just a behind-the-scenes thing to her, anyway. She might be wise. Our parents already despise us being wild rock stars with no morals. If they find out we're fucking our stepsister, they might never speak to us again.

The same might be representative of how the public would react.

Asking Aurora to suffer that judgment isn't fair. But living without her... That's it. That's the strange tangle inside my chest. I can deny what it is I want, but it's the nagging feeling that maybe I don't have to be alone in this world.

I mean, I'm never alone. I've got my brothers. I've got the band. But I've never connected with a woman. Aurora gets me. I don't even have to pretend to be broody.

That's what I want out of life...my sister.

Can we make it work? Can we be enough for her? She's so much. She's so full of life. So young. Damn. I've got ten years on her, and Calvin even more. Why can't I let this go?

"We've got a helluva mess on our hands. Is this thing with Aurora real?"

"What the fuck? You don't know if this is real? What do you think, it's just playtime?" Jack doesn't get where I'm coming from.

"It's real to me. Is that where we all stand?"

They all speak over each other, not giving space as they clamor to admit they've all caught feelings for her.

I try to steer the conversation. "Do we want to explore the cost of a relationship with Aurora, explain that it could cost her the relationship she has with our parents? She hasn't had time to come to terms with it like we have."

"Maybe if she hooks up with us, our parents will come around." Big D has to be joking.

"You've got to be kidding me," Jack says. "It would only be worse."

"Just trying to lighten the mood."

"We're a fucking thing, she just doesn't understand that yet." Calvin ends the discussion as he turns into the theater parking lot.

Our celebrity status and a promise to stay out of sight get us in the back door. Aurora's singing her heart out. She has the voice of an angel. She has everything of an angel.

I'm going to have to choose between being there for my brothers and the band, or being there for Aurora. Technically, the drummer's a pretty easy band member to swap out. Can I use that to my advantage?

I can focus on my personal work, turn it into something. Time to figure out if there's a market for Viking Fusion.

She runs through some spoken lines, sings a piece of the director's choosing, and does it well, then wraps up.

The director thanks her, and Calvin motions for us to step outside so we don't end up causing a scene if she catches us backstage. The four of us are leaning against the brick wall behind the auditorium when the door opens.

It's the sharp inhale of a sob, then the motion of her hand across her eyes, and the heave of her chest that wreck me. Shit. They're not happy tears. What's wrong? I rush to her.

"He asked if I could bring my brothers in to do a Master Class on stage presence."

I pull her into my chest. "We'll do it, but only if you want."

"No, don't interfere. Nothing at all from you guys. It makes me angry that he asked before giving me the part."

"If he wants us, he should reach out to our manager. Your audition is your space. I'm sorry people try to use you."

"It's not your fault."

I hold her tighter. "Now, explain why you left this morning. We worried—"

"I'm sorry, it was nerves. I thought...well, that if you were there, your presence would impact me. It happened anyway."

"I can't help that he's an ass, but I might be able to help with some of your anger."

"How?"

"It involves sex."

"What are we waiting for?"

"It's controversial to some people. It's called consensual non-consent. We'd agree on—"

"You mean CNC." Her eyes light up.

Fuck. She truly is an angel.

Fifteen

Aurora

I sang *Jingle Bells* while straightening the sheets of music on the coffee table. *Rudolph* and *Frosty* while spreading melted chocolate in the molds for hot chocolate bombs. And *Baby, It's Cold Outside* while strolling through their huge house familiarizing myself with the two-story layout.

Imagine the fun we could have as a family singing Christmas carols. Stopping by the fireplace, I sing *Chestnuts Roasting on an Open Fire*, although I don't think that's the actual name of it. The tiny tots with eyes aglow...I rub a hand on my belly. I could be pregnant. I want to be pregnant.

I love kids, but have I done something foolish? And not just me...my brothers never asked if I was on birth control. How did I go from thinking one night with them would be enough, to a few lessons, to anxiously awaiting CNC play?

I'm doing everything I can to act normal, including singing every Christmas carol I know while I wait for my brothers to make their move.

68

When he brought up CNC, I just about passed out. I've read about it as a safe way to act out what would normally be a terrible thing. Acting is the key. Everyone understands that I won't ever actually be in danger, but it's fair game to get aggressive.

We decided on the classic, *red*, as a safe word.

Jack asked about what to do if my mouth was full. We agreed that I would tap them with an arm or leg or tap the ground three times. Of course, that means they can't tie up my arms and legs and fill my mouth up at the same time, which I'm a little bummed about, but we'll do that in a different session.

The anticipation is killing me, but Travis insisted that I not know when to expect them to come for me. It'll be a better adrenaline surge.

We worked out a loose scenario and the guys are honing details amongst themselves.

Running out of classic Christmas carols, I break into Gwen Stefani and Blake Shelton's *You Make It Feel Like Christmas*.

I pull up the sheets on Jack's bed, wondering how many women he's had in here. Has he played this game before? What do I really know? I feel like I'm losing my heart to my brothers without seeing how it will ever work.

I've almost convinced our parents to come into town for Christmas, but a sexual relationship between us siblings would destroy them. It's too soon to worry about saying anything anyway. If our parents agree to dinner with all of us, we'll act normal. If I even know what that is anymore.

I fluff the pillows, then head downstairs to the kitchen. I love the open-concept home, with almost entire glass walls. So light and free in the middle of several gated acres. I don't have to flip the overhead lights on because of all the sunlight.

We confirmed that I'm fine if all of us end up together, but that I'm only okay with two of my holes being filled right now. One of those is my mouth. We'll work on the other hole a different time.

I handwash the single cup in the sink, dry it, and put it away.

Closing the cabinet, I turn toward the sink and stumble backward. Through the window, I see Calvin standing outside at the picnic table, arms folded and one ankle crossed over the other. Surely I would have noticed if he was there earlier.

When we were hanging out talking about our favorite shows, I told them how hot it was in *Good Girls* when Rio watches Beth through the kitchen window. Is that what they're doing?

Maybe. Maybe not. But the scene has begun. My heart races and I turn the water on to pretend wash my hands.

Footsteps approach from behind. I can barely breathe.

Calvin's watching but he won't have that great of a view since he can only see me from the waist up. I presume I'm about to get railed at the kitchen sink. Or not, if I resist.

"Is someone," I start to say looking over my shoulder and Travis closes in on me, his hips pinning me hard against the kitchen counter, his hands on either side.

"Hey, neighbor. Thought I'd come over and we could have some fun."

He's my neighbor, okay. How do I want to play this?

I'm so excited to be taken by my brothers again that it shocks me when Travis lifts one of his hands and whispers in my ear, "Run."

Despite all of my acting training, all of my improv sessions, all of my desire to do this... I freeze.

He leans away, and I'm trying to gather myself to do what he said, and a sharp slap on my ass is exactly the incentive I needed.

Every single muscle in my body tightens, for a split second before I sprint to the other side of the kitchen island. I grab the edge and stare him down. I hope I do this right. This is my chance to get aggressive and process my frustrations, but the promise of sex did that already.

I do love a chance to act, though. I cautiously lift one hand and say with a shaky voice, "I didn't let you in."

"You left the door unlocked." He rounds the island, and I don't freeze this time.

I bolt. He knows his house better than I do, but I weave through the long living room, around the couch, then the end table, trying to keep a piece of furniture between us at all times.

He slaps a hand on the back of the couch and launches himself over it.

I scream as he grabs my arm. Yanking with all my might, I slip away, positioning myself behind a plush chair.

"Leave her alone. I'm calling the police." Big D's voice from down the hall indicates he's on my side. Interesting.

"You want to call the cops? You'll have to come get your cell phone." Travis lunges toward the coffee table and grabs the phone Big D is heading for. "If she sucks my cock just right, I'll dial the number for you."

I'm tempted to drop to my knees, but movement out the back of the house draws my attention. Calvin has moved closer. He's on the back porch, his hands on an Adirondack chair, and he's smirking. Christ, that's seductive.

He lifts one hand and motions with his fingers for me to come outside. I doubt he's a good guy in this scenario.

Travis circles the far side of the chair, and I plan an escape, darting toward the front door. I throw it open and Jack steps out from behind a bush, rapidly approaching the door. The fire in his eyes is to die for.

But crap. There are so many of them. I detour to the stairs, grabbing the spindles so I don't overshoot. Travis's hand clamps over one of mine, his body presses into me from behind and my cheek hits our hands. Then he slaps my other hand back on the spindle.

Jack circles around us and runs onto the stairs, resting one knee on a higher step as he reaches over the rail and grabs my hair, forcing me to face his crotch.

"Hold this hand," Travis says to Jack, who complies, keeping me in place. Travis uses his now free hand to lift my skirt and promptly bites my ass.

"Help me, Doug!" I scream, hoping I read his role correctly.

"He can't help. You're ours now," Jack says while I hear a zipper being lowered behind me, followed by Travis shoving his pants down.

My eyes dart down to the outline of Jack's long, cock against his jeans. My panties are officially drenched.

"You want a closer look at my cock?"

"You can't make me." The crazy thing is I want them to make me. I've never been so aroused in my entire life.

"Leave my wife alone." Big D rushes in from the side, but Calvin knocks him into the wall.

That was rough. But he said *wife* and I can't get past it. My heart is about to explode. My pussy quivers at the thought of being married to them. The dream, the distant reality.

"Sit down and watch your wife take a real man's cock." That's Calvin slinging Doug into a chair. Then Calvin pulls his phone out of his pocket. "I'll make sure the neighbors can't hear."

Seconds later, Springsteen's *Santa Claus is Coming to Town* fills the house.

Jack lets go of my hair and Travis has taken control of both of my hands again. Jack strips his shirt then the rest of his clothes. His erection slaps his abs.

He positions himself on the stair so his cock is in my face and re-grabs my hair to make sure I see it. God, he's a work of art.

Travis slides his cock back and forth underneath me as Jack fists his cock, positions it between the spindles, and slaps it against my face, rubbing the tip over my lips. The salty pre-cum teases my tongue, the scent infiltrates my nose. I try to turn away but he won't let me.

I struggle but it's useless.

"Take a good look. When I'm done with your mouth, I'll flip you around and sink balls-deep into your cunt. Now open up like a good girl."

Without thinking, without resisting, I do. Dang it.

Jack slides in and out. Our hands cushion my face from the wooden spindles. I try not to moan in pleasure. My acting skills are getting a workout.

"Don't you dare move your hand." Travis waits for me to mumble agreement around Jack's cock before releasing one of my hands.

In one swift motion, he's using it to shove his cock into me. Two at a time. I love this. And I don't want to break anyone's cock, which I guess could happen, so I don't resist.

"I told you we'd have fun." Travis is right. The game is over. I'm not resisting. I'm loving every minute of their attention.

Even poor fake husband Doug, who's forced to watch instead of participate.

I moan and cry against Jack's shaft.

"Look how hot your wife is, getting double-teamed."

I'm confused by a scream from the front door while Calvin's bossing Doug.

"Stop that."

Oh no, it's my mom.

"Stop it right now." Our dad is with her.

Everyone's startled. Travis pulls back. The absence of Jack's cock in my mouth and Travis's from my pussy leave me abandoned and vulnerable. And yet they're both right here as shocked and probably embarrassed as I am. Humiliated.

Cold air graces my ass briefly before Travis pulls my skirt down. I force my body to stand. I don't want to turn around, but what good will it do to stay turned away?

The loud music stops abruptly. I turn to face the figurative music with my brothers.

"Aurora!" my mom shrieks, the level of horror in her voice etching itself into my memory.

Sixteen

Aurora

"Come with us young lady," our father says, reaching his hand out. My mother's already outside.

Jack pulls his jeans on, forgoing his underwear. "She doesn't have to go anywhere."

"It's okay, Jack. I'll go." I'll do whatever it takes to make this end.

Travis zips his pants, stands at my side, and speaks to our father. "She doesn't need saving. We're all adults."

Big D pipes in, "How the hell did you get in?"

"Calvin gave us the gate code, said we're always welcome."

Calvin paces away from us. "That was...over a year ago."

"We didn't realize we weren't welcome anymore. Your text said you wanted to see us. Take a good look. Now, we've got to get Aurora out of here before you corrupt her any more."

My four brothers try to intervene, but they're fired up. Letting them argue will only drive a bigger wedge in our family. I calmly say, "Let me handle this."

Then I scramble to figure out how as my parents drive me to their hotel. The drive is silent with the exception of Dad's loud, nostril-flaring breaths.

My phone keeps buzzing. The guys let me know I don't have to do this alone. Then a message from Cindy: *Having celebs in the family can suck*

She attached a video. I turn my volume down then play it. Lovely—footage from when the crowd rushed the stage after the concert. It's hard to make out, but in the background, my legs are wrapped around Jack. My face is nuzzled into his neck.

At least our parents don't use any social media.

When we finally get up to the room Dad paces, Mom sits in one chair and I take the other. Dad kicks off the inevitable. "You're young and impressionable."

"I'm an adult. I was as much a part of instigating it as they were. I gave my consent. We love each other. You don't understand what you interrupted." The more rapid-fire defensive statements I make, the flatter they fall.

"Oh, you love each other? Did they tell you that?" Dad asks.

Their proclamations streak through my mind.

He shakes his head. "And you believed them?"

I shrink into the cushions of the chair a little bit more.

"I never thought the four of them would stoop this low, especially Calvin."

My mom's voice is softer, and instead of anger, her words bear hurt. "Don't get tangled up in their world, honey. They make a lot of money and think that means they're successful, but they've thrown away their morals."

Dad interjects, "How did your last audition go?"

This question, on its own, could have a lot of different connotations. Coming from him, it pours alcohol straight into the wound.

He barely pauses. "Okay. Judging by your face, it didn't go well."

My face? Does he not understand what I'm going through? It doesn't matter if they outright say they're disgusted that they caught me having sex with my brothers.

He keeps going. "It might be time you get a real job. You've been disillusioned by your brothers that you can be a celebrity. But fame is fickle. Accounting...that's where it's at. A good, steady job."

"Yes," Mom says. "We tried to get your brothers to get real jobs, but they insisted on this music thing. They had a lot of really hard years. You were too young to realize how poor they were up until the last couple of years. We don't want that for you."

It's probably best if I let them speak their minds, but a ball of frustration grows inside of me. I wait as she purses her lips and takes in more air before continuing her monologue.

"And the fornication, you could end up pregnant."

My belly tightens. Now we're back on that topic. Not good.

"Whatever that was, Aurora, it's not normal. You have to value yourself. If we hadn't—"

"I get it. You don't approve of them. You don't approve of their music, but you don't even understand it, and you don't approve of my dreams, but that doesn't mean I don't have a right to explore them. And do even you realize what a big deal my brothers are?"

"Do you realize what a big deal incest is, honey?"

I can't believe Mom said that. Pointing out that it's not incest won't help.

"Honey, if people find out you've done that, you'll never be respected. It might even be hard to get a job as an accountant."

Too late for that warning, since the video surfaced. And why are my parents so convinced I should be an accountant? Sometimes I think Cindy should be their child instead of me. She's working on getting her accounting degree.

"That's my risk to take. I don't want to sit at a desk and look at numbers all day. I thrive on creativity. I want to inspire creativity in others. And I'll work whatever minimum wage jobs I have to while I establish myself. I get to make that choice. I get to pursue my dream. You don't get to stand in my way. They don't get to stand in my way. Nobody gets to tell me how to live my life."

I rush out the door, tears streaming down my face.

My words are much stronger than my soul, which is now crushed. Pieces of it fall with each teardrop as I rush to the elevator. I pull out my phone and open the rideshare app.

I need time alone. That's weird. I usually want to be with people. Travis is the loner of the family. Maybe I can learn from him. Time to go sit with myself.

Seventeen

Calvin

Of all the times I've told my parents I'd like to see them... It's not their fault. Any time in the last few days would have been risky.

Embracing reality doesn't help.

I wouldn't have thought they could think less of us, but now Rory's involved. Why the hell didn't she let us help her? How can I protect her from society's judgment if I can't control my own home?

Hating the answer, I slam my fist into the wall. My fingers ache as I rub them. Wouldn't be a smart move to break my fingers while we're on tour. Except that without a lead guitar, we could cancel. No. I'll do that of my own choosing if needed, not because I'm a dumbass who can't control my reactions.

Which reminds me that I need to think with my head. Rory wants to act, wants to have her own life, and wants to run a children's theater. That will mean she can't be on the road with us. I can't make her do it my way.

Fuck. If I want to show her that I respect her, I have to actually respect her. She deserves to be happy, even if it's not with my dick inside of her. Going on the world tour could be just what we need to give her space. How fast can our tour manager get venues booked?

I call my brothers into the living room.

"There's only one way I can see this working."

"All right, give it a go," Big D says.

"It's not going to work with Aurora."

They all rear up, but I motion for them to hear me out. "That horror on Mom and Dad's faces, we'll experience it elsewhere. Rory will experience it elsewhere. It's not something society's ready to accept. It's not going to advance her career."

Travis is sitting in the oversized chair Rory hid behind during our CNC play. He'd look like a fucking king if we hadn't just been destroyed. He leans forward. "So you're giving up on her?"

"Not giving up."

Jack stands in front of the couch and throws his arms out to the sides. "Sure sounds like it."

"I'm not giving up. I'm using logic and reason."

"How is your heart not in shambles?" Travis is furious.

"It is."

"Not if you can still think. I'm done with you and this fucking band. I'll do whatever it takes to be with her."

"I'm not thinking of us. I'm thinking of her. She wants to work with kids. How will she get people to trust her with their children if she's fucking her four brothers? Can you engage your brain enough to process that?"

"How can you feel—" Big D steps too close to me and I shove him back.

"This feels like absolute shit. She didn't even want us talking to Mom and Dad. She wanted to do it her own way because we always fuck things up for her. Let's all keep our dicks in our pants and not fuck her career up any more than we already have."

Eighteen

Travis

Calvin's trying to do the right thing, but the arrogant prick is still missing the point.

I say, "You guys are forgetting something pretty damn important."

Everybody looks at me.

"She wants to be heard and seen. She wants to be acknowledged for herself. Let her make the decision."

Our phones all buzz at the same time. Please let it be Aurora. We've texted her but gotten nothing back.

It's Mom: *Aurora left. Please let me know if she reaches out to you. I need to know that she's safe.*

At least there's a tinge of humanity in that woman.

None of us bother texting back. It would just open the door to criticism.

I usually sit back and let Calvin run the show. Sometimes Jack leads us on crazy adventures, or Doug charms us into shit. But this time it's too important. "We have to find her."

Jack volunteers, "I'll check her apartment."

Doug's on his phone. "I'm checking social media."

Calvin says, "I'll track down her friends."

We all head our different directions.

Aurora would be pissed that I use my celebrity to get into the otherwise closed children's theater. At least my intent is good. The second the door opens, the haunting words of my own song float around me. Some of the pronunciations are wrong, but it's unmistakable.

Have I lost my mind? I haven't shared that song with anyone.

I rush inside and stop short. I'm not hallucinating. It's Aurora.

I watch and listen from the back of the stage. A single spotlight shines on her. She's front and center, singing to a dark, empty auditorium, reading the music from her phone.

She's bringing it to life, tapping the drum beat on her thigh. Does she understand the words she's singing? The meaning? It's about devoting your entire soul to a person, your entire existence to serving that person. The person that you would travel to the ends of the earth for.

I text my brothers and let them know where she is. I don't disturb her. It's a little self-serving, hearing her sing my song. My fingers join her in tapping the drumbeats.

Aurora's singing has always been beautiful, but she might have perfect pitch. As the piece continues, I hum the baseline and I'm stoked over how haunting it sounds, how perfect we blend.

"Hey, Travis, I thought Aurora came alone," a man's voice says from my side. Dammit, there's where my celebrity gets me in trouble. It's a stagehand who's carrying a bundle of cables. I wave and he moves on.

Aurora's angelic tones float into the catwalk as she spins around. "I'm sorry, I took a picture of your song. I was singing it without permission."

I step out from the shadows. "You have my consent, always and forever."

"It's gorgeous, with an artistic simplicity. The kids would love performing something like this."

"Then let's do it with the kids. But I wrote it for you." I cross the stage and stop at the edge of the spotlight. My eyes drift to her belly. "Don't you think they're a little young?" My effort to make a joke is buried under uncertainty.

She grips her phone nervously at her waist. I reach into her spotlight, take her hands, and bring them to my lips.

"What if I am?" she whispers.

I step closer, covering her hands with mine. "I love you and I think that you are. We'll figure it out with you. Just don't shut us out."

"Deal, as long as you don't refer to the possible pregnancy in the plural again."

"Did I do that?" I mock disbelief.

"*They're* a little young?"

I wrap her in a hug, frustrated that my brothers arrive.

She pulls away. "What are you all doing here?"

"We were trying to find you. We didn't like the way that ended. How'd it go with the parents?" Doug asks.

"Exactly as you would think."

Doug exhales loudly. "First of all, we're sorry. And don't bother with telling us an apology's not necessary. Second of all, I love you, and—"

We cut him off as we talk over each other, vying for her to hear each of us express our love.

"Okay, okay, I get it...but our parents." She's young, hasn't even lived on her own for a year. It's a fair concern.

"Our parents have a lot of growing up to do. But that's what we want to ask you. We're willing to make this real. To be here for you, to have a relationship, for always and forever. But we need to know if that's what you want."

"Well, Travis says I'm pregnant, so we might not have a choice."

"Whoa." Calvin rests his hand on her shoulder. "You always have a choice. We're not forcing you into anything. But we hope you'll choose us."

"And there's one other thing you still have to choose." Big D looks proud of whatever he's scheming.

"*Still*?"

"Yeah, you haven't told us which position you prefer."

Nineteen

Big D

Not only did Aurora choose all of the positions, she chose all of us.

That sparked us to make some decisions pretty fast. No world tour, especially since she's probably pregnant. She agreed to pee on the stick today, but has already moved in. And adding her to our band, we're exploring Travis's Viking stuff.

I'm at my home keyboard, making sure I've memorized the Viking piece we're about to head to the stage to try out when my phone dings.

"I got the new logo back from the designer," I call out and wait while my siblings head over. Aurora doesn't know the logo's a joke. And I didn't expect the designer to turn it around by Christmas.

"A new logo?" She studies my phone screen. "You changed The Rebels to The Revels?"

Jack says, "It seems fitting since we're doing a lot more celebrating than rebelling these days."

Calvin continues the joke. "The oversized V in the Viking font sets our new tone."

I pull her onto my lap, struggling to sound serious. "Symbolic of our sister giving us her V-card."

She slaps her hands over her mouth and blushes. "Absolutely not."

"But you're our inspiration." Travis's sincerity shines through.

She slides her hands over her face, takes a few deep breaths, then says, "Since we're honest...I have to admit, I like it."

"Really?" I hope she does. It came out better than I expected.

"Yeah, it's—"

"We did it as a joke," I clarify.

"But it's great."

"It's us," Travis says. He's right.

Hugs ensue, as they often do, then Calvin reminds us, "We can't keep the stagehands away from their families too long on Christmas Eve."

When Aurora shared a Viking demo we threw together with her co-workers at the theater, they insisted we try it out on stage.

"They aren't expecting us for one more hour." I kiss Aurora's neck, sending shivers through her.

"Time for a quickie?" Jack asks.

"As long as there's time for me to clean up." She strides across the room, tossing clothes as she heads to the Christmas tree she insisted we put up, tinsel and all.

Calvin throws a blanket on the carpet then gets rid of his own clothes. She drops to her knees, leans forward, stretching her hands out as she lowers herself to the blanket. Her ass looks great in the twinkling lights of the Christmas tree, but I think it looks great everywhere.

She looks great everywhere, no additional sparkle needed.

Rolling onto her back, she smiles up at us. We drop to our knees around her, everyone content with where they are. I'm the lucky one at her feet. After kissing my way up her legs, I lavish my love on her with my mouth, then bury my cock inside of her.

Jack has his cock in her mouth, getting the benefit of her moans vibrating on his shaft. Calvin and Travis cover her body with their attention.

Watching Aurora surrender so freely to all of us while she comes on my cock fills my heart and soul with more joy than I thought was possible. And watching her take each of my brothers in turn solidifies how intensely I needed this...a family that truly loves each other.

Calvin makes sure that we are cleaned up, get to the theater, and finish our setup, even adding Viking face paint, on time. Everyone knows their role.

Travis starts with a monotone hum amidst total darkness. Aurora joins softly, her voice floating above his in a perfect octave. They build over a long, slow crescendo, before Travis adds the beat, increasing the tempo.

I sneak in on the keyboard, sliding the volume up slowly. We want it to grow into the audience's awareness. Then Jack hits a single note on his bass, letting it fade before repeating it.

Everything builds to the big entry with Aurora shifting to the chant and Calvin coming in on lead guitar. The stagehands time the spotlight perfectly, shining it on her.

The rest of us linger in the dark background; we're incidentals, put on this earth to nurture her.

When we wrap up the set, Jack disappears briefly then comes back without the face paint.

He greets Aurora with a hug. "Let's get home to celebrate Christmas."

"You cleaned up awful fast," she says.

"I'm only that guy on stage. I'm not the bad boy. I'm not a Viking whatever. I'm yours, and I want to make sure you see that."

"I do, Jack. I see the real you. I also know what you're really in a hurry for."

We've waited for this day. We put it on the calendar and promised not to bug Aurora until today came. We head straight to the store and let her go inside and get the pregnancy test of her choosing. Then Calvin drives us home and we wait anxiously while she pees on that little stick.

It's agony waiting, but when the little pink plus shows up, I watch her expression.

A smile. Fuck yeah!

"Dibs on the kids calling me Pappy." I'm laughing so hard I can barely finish the line.

"Have you been waiting this whole time to say that?" Calvin doesn't appreciate the humor."

"Yep, because it means I got her pregnant."

"You?" she asks.

"A guy can dream." And thank goodness I did. She's ours forever and she's truly happy about it.

Epilogue

Aurora

Staring at the heavy curtain on the stage, I'm tickled by all of the buzz around me in the audience. Parents are eager to see their children perform. I've achieved my dream with the help of my brothers, not in spite of them.

They bought out the theater, allowing the current director an easy, early retirement. And with all of our changes, the guys finished out the shows they were committed to and helped me put on our first children's theater performance.

It's even more nerve-wracking than I expected, but they made me promise to rest and trust that they could handle showtime, since the twins have been giving my belly a workout.

My brothers were theater kids growing up. They remember the fun. And they've spent the last several months brushing up on the details.

I rub my hand over my giant belly. This very well could be one of my last outings.

"Is the baby kicking?" my mom asks. "It's not time, is it?"

My dad winks. "I'm eager to meet the grandkids, but I don't think the show can go on if your whole family has to head to the hospital."

My whole family...my heart melts. I wasn't sure if we'd ever get to this day. Our parents couldn't understand how we could be attracted to each other. My brothers are older, and all of them sharing one woman?

I understand it sounds weird, but it's us.

Once our parents saw that we were dedicated to each other and that we would risk losing them before we would risk losing our crazy ensemble, they had to make a choice.

"Not time to go yet, Dad." I pat his leg.

"This is going to be amazing," Dad says.

"The guys have to put on the show before we give accolades."

And they do. The show is a stellar success. The guys are a little ragged, but we meet backstage afterward.

Travis emceed the evening, no more hiding behind his drums being dark and broody. He had the crowd lit up before the show even started.

Calvin flicks a piece of glitter off his phone as he shows us a picture of his handiwork. He fixed a tutu with a stapler. Very clever. He realizes the glitter is stuck to his fingertip, wipes it on my cheek, and winks. I do love to sparkle.

And Big Doug, as he's called by the kids, did a fabulous job on keys for the musical numbers, even seamlessly helping the kid who mixed up his lyrics get back on track.

I'm doubled over my belly laughing as Jack wraps up about one of the little boys who came crying to him that someone had stepped on his kazoo. Jack saved the day with duct tape.

They're going to make great dads. And maybe sooner rather than later.

Intense pain shoots through my midsection. I've been having Braxton Hicks, but this is more intense.

Travis rubs my back. "And we couldn't have done any of this without Aurora. Shall we go celebrate?"

I lift up and meet his eyes. "Sorry to force a change of plans, but we better go to the hospital."

My mom laughs. "Honey, you always know how to steal the show."

The guys help me into the SUV and our parents follow us to the hospital.

Between contractions, I say, "You guys did amazing tonight."

Calvin meets my eyes in the rear-view mirror. "We never could have done that without you. Love you, Aurora."

And we live happily ever after!

Would you like a little more **Carols and Consent**?

If you'd like to read a deleted scene where the brothers agonize over what to do about Aurora, grab this BONUS SCENE by signing up for my newsletter.

Once you subscribe, I'll keep you up to date on my stories, sales, and other Super Hot content you won't want to miss!
Visit my website: https://SylvieHaas.com
And true to my initials, SHhhh, I'll let it be our little secret.

Sugar D's Speed Dating
Why Choose the Bodyguards
Why Choose the Stepbrothers
Why Choose the Billionaires
Why Choose the Beards

Eggplant Canyon Phase 2: The Bratva Moves In
Virgin and the Bratva
Fake Engagement and the Bratva
Secret Baby and the Bratva
and more...

Acknowledgments

Christy...the verdict is still out on whether I love you or hate you for that Pinterest link for hot chocolate bombs! And if I fail to write any more books, I'm probably busy trying every recipe I can find. Or I'm in a sugar coma! Cross your fingers that I survive this rabbit hole!

About the Author

Sylvie Haas obsesses over dirty-talking heroes who fall hard and fast for the woman of their dreams. And you'll find multiple heroes in one book because she has such a hard time making the heroine choose one possessive guy.

On most days, you can find Sylvie with the wind in her hair, her fingers on the keyboard, and her mind in the gutter as she thinks up new places her characters can get frisky.

Sylvie's books will always deliver a happily ever after, and even though they're short, they'll leave you satisfied!

If you haven't signed up for her newsletter yet, there's still room. The more the merrier!

https://SylvieHaas.com

www.ingramcontent.com/pod-product-compliance
Lightning Source LLC
Chambersburg PA
CBHW010934120626
46552CB00010B/3259

9 781950 166657